NOW I KNOW™
Healthy Eat[ing]

by MELVIN AND GILDA BERGER

SCHOLASTIC INC.

New York   Toronto   London   Auckland   Sydney
Mexico City   New Delhi   Hong Kong   Buenos Aires

What keeps you healthy?

Healthy eating!
You need food to live.

5

Grains give you energy.

Wheat, corn, and rice are grains.

Grains come from plants.

Mmmm. Good!

Eat grains at every meal.

Vegetables keep you healthy.

DID YOU KNOW?

Carrots are roots; lettuce is leaves.

Vegetables come from plants.

Crunch! Celery is a great snack.

Eat vegetables every day.

Fruits help keep you healthy.

Fruits also come from plants.

ZOOM!

15

Grapes are good and juicy.

Eat fruit at every meal.

Meat keeps you strong.
Nuts and beans do, too.

DID YOU KNOW?
We get beef from cattle and pork from pigs.

Meat comes from land animals.

Open wide!

Eat some meat, nuts, or beans every day.

Seafood also helps keep you strong.

Seafood comes from
animals that live in water.

DID YOU KNOW?

The egg yolk has lots of vitamins.

ZOOM!

Chickens give us eggs.

It's fun to cook with eggs.

Milk helps you grow.
Milk is used to make butter,
cheese, and ice cream.

Cows give us milk.

Milk is a great drink.

Drink three glasses of milk every day.

Which healthy foods do you like to eat?

Healthy eating makes
you feel so-o-o good!

GLOSSARY

Beans: Large seeds or pods of plants that are often good to eat.

Energy: The strength to do things without getting tired.

Fit: To be healthy and strong.

Grains: The seeds of cereal plants.

Healthy: Feeling fit and well.

Leaves: The parts of plants that grow out from the stems.

Plants: Living things that can make food from the energy of the sun.

Roots: The parts of plants that grow under the ground.

Seafood: Fish and shellfish that are good to eat.

Stems: The parts of plants from which the leaves and flowers grow.